Dramatis Personæ

Duncan
King of Scotland

Malcolm
Son of Duncan

Donalbain
Son of Duncan

Macduff
Nobleman of Scotland

Lenox
Nobleman of Scotland

Rosse
Nobleman of Scotland

Lady Macbeth
Wife of Macbeth

Lady Macduff
Wife of Macduff

Siward *Earl of Northumberland,*
General of the English forces

**A Gentlewoman attending
to Lady Macbeth**

Seyton
An officer attending to Macbeth

An English Doctor

A Scottish Doctor

A Porter

An Old Man

Murderer 1

Murderer 2

Murderer 3

Editor in Chief: Clive Bryant

Macbeth: The Graphic Novel
Original Text Version

William Shakespeare

First published: February 2008
Reprinted: December 2008

Published by: Classical Comics Ltd
Copyright ©2008 Classical Comics Ltd.

Acknowledgments: Every effort has been made to trace copyright holders of
material reproduced in this book. Any rights not acknowledged here will be
acknowledged in subsequent editions if notice is given to Classical Comics Ltd.

Images on pages 3 & 6 reproduced with the kind permission of
the Trustees of the National Library of Scotland. © National Library of Scotland.

All enquiries should be addressed to:
Classical Comics Ltd.
PO Box 7280
Litchborough
Towcester
NN12 9AR
United Kingdom
Tel: 0845 812 3000

info@classicalcomics.com
www.classicalcomics.com

ISBN: 978-1-906332-03-7

Printed in Italy by Printer Trento S.r.l. using vegetable inks.

The book in your hands is made from paper
certified by FSC (Forest Stewardship Council) CQ-COC-000012.

Printer Trento S.r.l. is also certified ISO 14001:2004 (Environmental Management Standard).

The rights of John McDonald, Jon Haward, Nigel Dobbyn and Gary Erskine
to be identified as the artists of this work have been asserted in accordance with
the Copyright, Designs and Patents Act 1988 sections 77 and 78.

Dramatis Personæ

Macbeth
General in the King's Army

Banquo
General in the King's Army

The Ghost of Banquo

Menteth
Nobleman of Scotland

Angus
Nobleman of Scotland

Cathness
Nobleman of Scotland

Young Siward
Son of Siward

Fleance
Son of Banquo

Boy
Son of Macduff

Witch 1

Witch 2

Witch 3

and Lords, Ladies,
Officers, Soldiers,
Messengers, Attendants
and Apparitions.

Hecate
The "Queen" Witch

Prologue

Scotland in the year 1040.

King Duncan has ruled the land for six years, ever since the death of his grandfather, Malcolm II. Duncan is a good king, but even under his kind and gentle ruling, Scotland is far from being a settled nation.

For centuries, following the departure of the Romans, the land has been split in two — with bands of Vikings in the north, and tribes of Saxons in the south. It's a barbaric land. Each local tribe has its own strong leader: men relying on the strength of their sword arm for honours and often having to fight for their very survival.

But the country is changing. With the reign of King Duncan came a rare promise of unity amongst the tribes to create a single, Scottish nation ruled by a single Scottish King. However, not everyone welcomes this peace. Some chieftains want to maintain their independence and continue to rebel against the King, often joining forces with warriors from other tribes and from other countries such as Ireland and Norway; and there are even some chieftains who would like to claim the title of King of Scotland for themselves.

To defend his crown, and to maintain order in his land, King Duncan commands a powerful army, led by noblemen who are experienced in the ways of war - and the mightiest and most trusted of these noblemen is King Duncan's cousin, the Thane of Glamis, otherwise known as…

…Macbeth.

A Note on Pronunciation

As you go through this Original Text version, you will notice how some words that usually end in "-ed" are written "-d" whereas others are written out in full.

Shakespeare wrote much of his plays in verse, where the rhythm of the speech formed strings of "iambic pentameters", each line being five pairs of syllables, with the second syllable in each pair being the most dominant in the rhythm.

To help with enunciation and voice projection in early theatres, words that ended with "-ed" had that last syllable accented – unless to do so would have spoiled the iambic rhythm, in which case it was spoken just as we say the word today.

This speech by Macbeth:

Accursed be that tongue that tells me so,

would have been said as:

Accurse-ed be that tongue that tells me so,

so that the syllable pairs (five of them in the line) are correct in number and in emphasis (if you say it as "accurs'd" you'll see how the rhythm of the line is destroyed).

Whereas:

And damn'd be him that first cries, "Hold enough!"

cannot be pronounced "dam-ned" because to do so would give eleven syllables in the line, and would not allow the right emphasis to be placed on each syllable.

In short, whenever you see a word ending "-ed" it should have its 'e' pronounced to preserve the rhythm of the speech.

FROM *FIFE*, GREAT KING; WHERE THE *NORWEYAN BANNERS* FLOUT THE SKY AND FAN OUR PEOPLE COLD. *NORWAY HIMSELF*, WITH TERRIBLE NUMBERS, ASSISTED BY THAT MOST DISLOYAL TRAITOR, *THE THANE OF CAWDOR*, BEGAN A DISMAL CONFLICT;

TILL THAT *BELLONA'S BRIDEGROOM*, LAPP'D IN PROOF, CONFRONTED HIM WITH SELF-COMPARISONS, POINT AGAINST POINT REBELLIOUS, ARM 'GAINST ARM, CURBING HIS LAVISH SPIRIT: AND, TO CONCLUDE, THE *VICTORY* FELL ON *US*;

GREAT HAPPINESS!

THAT NOW *SWENO*, THE NORWAYS' KING, CRAVES *COMPOSITION;* NOR WOULD WE DEIGN HIM BURIAL OF HIS MEN TILL HE DISBURSED AT SAINT COLME'S INCH *TEN THOUSAND DOLLARS* TO OUR GENERAL USE.

NO MORE THAT THANE OF CAWDOR SHALL DECEIVE OUR BOSOM INTEREST. -- GO PRONOUNCE HIS PRESENT DEATH, AND WITH HIS *FORMER TITLE* GREET MACBETH.

I'LL SEE IT DONE.

WHAT HE HATH *LOST*, NOBLE *MACBETH* HATH *WON*.

A Scottish heath...

WHERE HAST THOU BEEN, SISTER?

KILLING SWINE.

SISTER, WHERE THOU?

A SAILOR'S WIFE HAD **CHESTNUTS** IN HER LAP, AND MOUNCH'D, AND MOUNCH'D, AND MOUNCH'D:

'GIVE ME,' QUOTH I: — 'AROINT THEE, WITCH!' THE RUMP-FED RONYON CRIES.

HER HUSBAND'S TO **ALEPPO** GONE, MASTER O' THE TIGER: BUT IN A SIEVE I'LL THITHER SAIL, AND, LIKE A RAT WITHOUT A TAIL; I'LL DO, I'LL DO, AND I'LL DO.

I'LL GIVE THEE A WIND.

TH'ART KIND.

AND I ANOTHER.

LOOK, HOW OUR PARTNER'S *RAPT*.

IF CHANCE WILL HAVE ME *KING,* WHY, CHANCE MAY *CROWN* ME, WITHOUT MY STIR.

NEW HONOURS COME UPON HIM, LIKE OUR *STRANGE GARMENTS,* CLEAVE NOT TO THEIR MOULD, BUT WITH THE AID OF *USE.*

COME WHAT COME MAY, TIME AND THE HOUR RUNS THROUGH THE *ROUGHEST* DAY.

WORTHY MACBETH, WE STAY UPON YOUR *LEISURE.*

GIVE ME YOUR FAVOUR: MY *DULL BRAIN* WAS WROUGHT WITH THINGS *FORGOTTEN.* KIND GENTLEMEN, YOUR PAINS ARE REGISTER'D WHERE EVERY DAY I TURN THE LEAF TO READ THEM. -- LET US TOWARD THE *KING.*

THINK UPON WHAT HATH CHANC'D; AND AT MORE TIME, THE INTERIM HAVING WEIGH'D IT, LET US SPEAK OUR *FREE HEARTS* EACH TO OTHER.

VERY GLADLY.

TILL THEN, *ENOUGH.*

COME, FRIENDS.

The King's Palace at Forres. The rebellion dealt with, King Duncan waits for Macbeth and Banquo...

IS EXECUTION DONE ON *CAWDOR?* ARE NOT THOSE IN COMMISSION YET RETURN'D?

MY LIEGE, THEY ARE NOT YET COME BACK; BUT I HAVE SPOKE WITH ONE THAT *SAW* HIM DIE: WHO DID REPORT, THAT VERY *FRANKLY* HE CONFESS'D HIS *TREASONS*, IMPLOR'D YOUR HIGHNESS' *PARDON*, AND SET FORTH A *DEEP REPENTANCE.*

NOTHING IN HIS LIFE BECAME HIM LIKE THE *LEAVING* IT: HE DIED AS ONE THAT HAD BEEN *STUDIED* IN HIS DEATH, TO THROW AWAY THE DEAREST THING HE OW'D, AS 'TWERE A *CARELESS TRIFLE.*

THERE'S NO ART TO FIND THE *MIND'S CONSTRUCTION* IN THE *FACE:*

HE WAS A *GENTLEMAN* ON WHOM I BUILT AN ABSOLUTE TRUST.

O *WORTHIEST* COUSIN!

THE SIN OF MY INGRATITUDE EVEN NOW WAS *HEAVY* ON ME. THOU ART SO FAR BEFORE, THAT SWIFTEST WING OF RECOMPENSE IS SLOW TO OVERTAKE THEE: 'WOULD THOU HADST LESS DESERV'D, THAT THE PROPORTION BOTH OF THANKS AND PAYMENT MIGHT HAVE BEEN MINE! ONLY I HAVE LEFT TO SAY, MORE IS THY *DUE* THAN MORE THAN ALL CAN *PAY.*

THE SERVICE AND THE LOYALTY I OWE, IN DOING IT, PAYS *ITSELF.* YOUR *HIGHNESS'* PART IS TO *RECEIVE* OUR DUTIES;

AND OUR DUTIES ARE TO YOUR *THRONE AND STATE, CHILDREN AND SERVANTS;* WHICH DO BUT WHAT THEY SHOULD, BY DOING EVERY THING SAFE TOWARD YOUR *LOVE AND HONOUR.*

WELCOME HITHER: I HAVE BEGUN TO *PLANT* THEE, AND WILL LABOUR TO MAKE THEE FULL OF *GROWING.*

NOBLE BANQUO, THAT HAST NO LESS DESERV'D, NOR MUST BE KNOWN NO LESS TO HAVE DONE SO, LET ME *INFOLD* THEE, AND HOLD THEE TO MY *HEART.*

THERE IF I GROW, THE *HARVEST* IS YOUR *OWN.*

MY PLENTEOUS *JOYS*, WANTON IN FULNESS, SEEK TO HIDE THEMSELVES IN DROPS OF *SORROW.*

SONS, KINSMEN, THANES, AND YOU WHOSE PLACES ARE THE NEAREST, KNOW, WE WILL ESTABLISH OUR ESTATE UPON OUR ELDEST, *MALCOLM;* WHOM WE NAME HEREAFTER THE *PRINCE OF CUMBERLAND;* WHICH HONOUR MUST NOT, UNACCOMPANIED, INVEST HIM ONLY, BUT SIGNS OF NOBLENESS, LIKE STARS, SHALL SHINE ON *ALL* DESERVERS.

FROM HENCE TO *INVERNESS*, AND BIND US *FURTHER* TO YOU.

THE *REST* IS LABOUR, WHICH IS NOT US'D FOR YOU: I'LL BE *MYSELF* THE HARBINGER, AND MAKE *JOYFUL* THE HEARING OF MY WIFE WITH YOUR *APPROACH*; SO, HUMBLY TAKE MY LEAVE.

THE *PRINCE OF CUMBERLAND!* -- THAT IS A STEP, ON WHICH I MUST *FALL DOWN*, OR ELSE *O'ERLEAP*, FOR IN MY WAY IT LIES. STARS, HIDE YOUR FIRES!

LET NOT LIGHT SEE MY BLACK AND DEEP DESIRES; THE EYE WINK AT THE HAND; YET LET THAT BE, WHICH THE EYE FEARS, WHEN IT IS DONE, TO SEE.

MY *WORTHY CAWDOR!*

TRUE, WORTHY BANQUO: HE IS FULL SO *VALIANT* AND IN HIS COMMENDATIONS I AM FED; IT IS A *BANQUET* TO ME.

LET US AFTER HIM, WHOSE CARE IS GONE BEFORE TO BID US WELCOME: IT IS A *PEERLESS* KINSMAN.

Act One
Scene Five

At Macbeth's castle, in Inverness, Lady Macbeth receives news from her husband...

"THEY MET ME IN THE DAY OF SUCCESS; AND I HAVE LEARN'D BY THE PERFECT'ST REPORT, THEY HAVE MORE IN THEM THAN *MORTAL KNOWLEDGE.*

WHEN I BURN'D IN DESIRE TO QUESTION THEM FURTHER, THEY MADE THEMSELVES *AIR*, INTO WHICH THEY VANISH'D."

"WHILES I STOOD RAPT IN THE *WONDER* OF IT, CAME MISSIVES FROM THE KING, WHO ALL-HAIL'D ME, *"THANE OF CAWDOR;"* BY WHICH TITLE, BEFORE, THESE WEIRD SISTERS *SALUTED* ME, AND REFERR'D ME TO THE COMING ON O' TIME, WITH *"HAIL, KING THAT SHALT BE!"*

"THIS HAVE I THOUGHT GOOD TO DELIVER THEE, MY DEAREST PARTNER OF GREATNESS, THAT THOU MIGHT'ST NOT LOSE THE DUES OF *REJOICING*, BY BEING IGNORANT OF WHAT *GREATNESS* IS PROMIS'D THEE. LAY IT TO THY *HEART*, AND FAREWELL."

GLAMIS THOU ART, AND *CAWDOR*; AND SHALT BE WHAT THOU ART PROMIS'D -- YET DO I FEAR THY *NATURE*: IT IS TOO FULL O' THE *MILK OF HUMAN KINDNESS*, TO CATCH THE NEAREST WAY. THOU WOULDST BE *GREAT*; ART NOT WITHOUT *AMBITION*, BUT WITHOUT THE *ILLNESS* SHOULD *ATTEND* IT:

WHAT THOU WOULDST *HIGHLY*, THAT WOULDST THOU *HOLILY*; WOULDST NOT PLAY *FALSE*, AND YET WOULDST W*RONGLY WIN*; THOU'DST HAVE, GREAT GLAMIS, THAT WHICH CRIES, "THUS THOU MUST DO, IF THOU HAVE IT;" AND THAT WHICH RATHER THOU DOST *FEAR* TO DO THAN WISHEST SHOULD BE *UNDONE.*

HIE THEE HITHER, THAT I MAY POUR MY *SPIRITS* IN THINE EAR, AND CHASTISE WITH THE VALOUR OF MY TONGUE ALL THAT IMPEDES THEE FROM THE *GOLDEN ROUND*, WHICH FATE AND METAPHYSICAL AID DOTH SEEM TO HAVE THEE *CROWN'D* WITHAL.

GREAT *GLAMIS*! WORTHY *CAWDOR*! GREATER THAN BOTH, BY THE ALL-HAIL HEREAFTER!

THY *LETTERS* HAVE TRANSPORTED ME *BEYOND* THIS IGNORANT PRESENT, AND I FEEL NOW THE *FUTURE* IN THE INSTANT.

MY DEAREST LOVE, *DUNCAN* COMES HERE TO-NIGHT.

AND WHEN GOES HE *HENCE?*

TO-MORROW, AS HE PURPOSES.

O, NEVER SHALL SUN THAT MORROW SEE! YOUR *FACE*, MY THANE, IS AS A *BOOK* WHERE MEN MAY READ *STRANGE MATTERS.* TO *BEGUILE* THE TIME, *LOOK* LIKE THE TIME; BEAR *WELCOME* IN YOUR EYE, YOUR HAND, YOUR TONGUE: LOOK LIKE THE *INNOCENT FLOWER,*

BUT BE THE *SERPENT* UNDER'T. HE THAT'S COMING MUST BE *PROVIDED* FOR: AND YOU SHALL PUT THIS NIGHT'S GREAT BUSINESS INTO *MY* DISPATCH;

WHICH SHALL TO ALL OUR NIGHTS AND DAYS TO COME GIVE SOLELY *SOVEREIGN SWAY* AND *MASTERDOM.*

WE WILL SPEAK FURTHER.

ONLY LOOK UP *CLEAR;* TO ALTER *FAVOUR* EVER IS TO *FEAR.* LEAVE ALL THE REST TO *ME.*

Act One
Scene Six

The King has arrived at Macbeth's castle in Inverness...

THIS CASTLE HATH A *PLEASANT* SEAT; THE AIR NIMBLY AND SWEETLY RECOMMENDS ITSELF UNTO OUR GENTLE SENSES.

THIS GUEST OF SUMMER, THE TEMPLE-HAUNTING *MARTLET*, DOES APPROVE, BY HIS LOV'D MANSIONRY, THAT THE HEAVEN'S BREATH SMELLS *WOOINGLY* HERE: NO JUTTY, FRIEZE, BUTTRESS, NOR COIGN OF VANTAGE, BUT THIS BIRD HATH MADE HIS *PENDENT BED* AND *PROCREANT CRADLE*:

WHERE THEY MOST BREED AND HAUNT, I HAVE OBSERV'D, THE AIR IS *DELICATE*.

HOW *NOW!* WHAT NEWS?

HE HAS ALMOST *SUPP'D.* WHY HAVE YOU LEFT THE CHAMBER?

HATH HE *ASK'D* FOR ME?

KNOW YOU NOT, HE HAS?

WE WILL PROCEED *NO FURTHER* IN THIS BUSINESS: HE HATH *HONOUR'D* ME OF LATE; AND I HAVE BOUGHT *GOLDEN OPINIONS* FROM ALL SORTS OF PEOPLE, WHICH WOULD BE WORN NOW IN THEIR NEWEST GLOSS, NOT *CAST ASIDE* SO SOON.

WAS THE HOPE *DRUNK* WHEREIN YOU DRESS'D YOURSELF? HATH IT *SLEPT* SINCE, AND *WAKES* IT NOW, TO LOOK SO GREEN AND PALE AT WHAT IT DID SO FREELY? FROM THIS TIME SUCH I *ACCOUNT* THY LOVE.

ART THOU *AFEARD* TO BE THE SAME IN THINE OWN ACT AND VALOUR, AS THOU ART IN DESIRE? WOULDST THOU HAVE THAT WHICH THOU ESTEEM'ST THE ORNAMENT OF LIFE, AND LIVE A *COWARD* IN THINE OWN ESTEEM, LETTING 'I DARE NOT' WAIT UPON 'I WOULD,' LIKE THE POOR *CAT* I' THE ADAGE?

PR'YTHEE, PEACE. I DARE DO *ALL* THAT MAY BECOME A MAN; WHO DARES DO *MORE*, IS *NONE*.

WHAT *BEAST* WAS'T, THEN, THAT MADE YOU *BREAK* THIS ENTERPRISE TO ME? WHEN YOU DURST DO IT, THEN YOU WERE A *MAN*; AND, TO BE MORE THAN WHAT YOU WERE, YOU WOULD BE SO MUCH *MORE* THE MAN. NOR TIME, NOR PLACE, DID THEN ADHERE, AND YET YOU WOULD MAKE *BOTH*:

THEY HAVE *MADE* THEMSELVES, AND THAT THEIR FITNESS NOW DOES *UNMAKE* YOU.

I HAVE GIVEN *SUCK*, AND KNOW HOW *TENDER* 'TIS TO LOVE THE BABE THAT *MILKS* ME: I WOULD, WHILE IT WAS SMILING IN MY FACE, HAVE PLUCK'D MY *NIPPLE* FROM HIS *BONELESS GUMS*, AND DASH'D THE *BRAINS* OUT, HAD I SO SWORN AS YOU HAVE DONE TO THIS.

IF WE SHOULD *FAIL*?

WE FAIL! BUT SCREW YOUR COURAGE TO THE *STICKING-PLACE*, AND WE'LL *NOT* FAIL.

THERE'S NO SUCH THING. IT IS THE **BLOODY BUSINESS** WHICH INFORMS THUS TO MINE EYES.

NOW O'ER THE ONE HALF-WORLD NATURE SEEMS **DEAD**, AND **WICKED DREAMS** ABUSE THE CURTAIN'D SLEEP: WITCHCRAFT CELEBRATES PALE **HECATE'S** OFFERINGS; AND WITHER'D **MURDER**, ALARUM'D BY HIS SENTINEL, THE WOLF, WHOSE HOWL'S HIS WATCH, THUS WITH HIS STEALTHY PACE, WITH TARQUIN'S RAVISHING STRIDES, TOWARDS HIS DESIGN MOVES LIKE A **GHOST**.

DONG! DONG!

THOU SURE AND FIRM-SET EARTH, HEAR NOT MY **STEPS**, WHICH WAY THEY WALK, FOR FEAR THY VERY **STONES** PRATE OF MY WHERE-ABOUT, AND TAKE THE PRESENT HORROR FROM THE TIME, WHICH NOW SUITS WITH IT.

WHILES I **THREAT**, HE **LIVES**: WORDS TO THE HEAT OF DEEDS **TOO COLD BREATH** GIVES.

I **GO**, AND IT IS **DONE**; THE **BELL** INVITES ME. HEAR IT **NOT**, DUNCAN; FOR IT IS A KNELL THAT SUMMONS THEE TO **HEAVEN**, OR TO **HELL**.

Act Two
Scene Two

A while later...

THAT WHICH HATH MADE THEM *DRUNK* HATH MADE ME *BOLD*: WHAT HATH QUENCH'D *THEM* HATH GIVEN *ME* FIRE.

HARK! *PEACE!*

IT WAS THE *OWL* THAT SHRIEK'D, THE *FATAL BELLMAN*, WHICH GIVES THE STERN'ST GOOD-NIGHT. HE IS *ABOUT* IT. THE *DOORS* ARE *OPEN*: AND THE *SURFEITED GROOMS* DO MOCK THEIR CHARGE WITH *SNORES*: I HAVE *DRUGG'D* THEIR *POSSETS*, THAT DEATH AND NATURE DO CONTEND ABOUT THEM, WHETHER THEY *LIVE*, OR *DIE*.

WHO'S THERE? -- *WHAT, HO!*

ALACK, I AM AFRAID THEY HAVE *AWAK'D*, AND 'TIS *NOT DONE*: -- THE ATTEMPT AND NOT THE DEED *CONFOUNDS* US.

HARK! -- I LAID THEIR *DAGGERS* READY; HE COULD NOT *MISS* THEM. -- HAD HE NOT RESEMBLED MY *FATHER* AS HE SLEPT, *I* HAD DONE'T.

MY HUSBAND!

I HAVE *DONE* THE DEED. -- DIDST THOU NOT HEAR A *NOISE?*

I HEARD THE *OWL* SCREAM, AND THE *CRICKETS* CRY. DID NOT YOU *SPEAK?*

ONE CRIED, *'GOD BLESS US!'* AND *'AMEN,'* THE *OTHER,* AS THEY HAD SEEN ME WITH THESE *HANGMAN'S HANDS.* LIST'NING THEIR FEAR, I COULD NOT SAY, *'AMEN,'* WHEN THEY DID SAY, *'GOD BLESS US.'*

CONSIDER IT NOT SO *DEEPLY.*

BUT WHEREFORE COULD NOT I PRONOUNCE 'AMEN'? I HAD *MOST NEED* OF *BLESSING,* AND 'AMEN' STUCK IN MY *THROAT.*

THESE DEEDS MUST NOT BE *THOUGHT AFTER* THESE WAYS; SO, IT WILL MAKE US *MAD.*

METHOUGHT, I HEARD A VOICE CRY, *'SLEEP NO MORE! MACBETH DOES MURDER* SLEEP,'

THE *INNOCENT* SLEEP; SLEEP, THAT KNITS UP THE RAVELL'D SLEAVE OF *CARE,* THE *DEATH* OF EACH DAY'S *LIFE,* SORE LABOUR'S *BATH, BALM* OF *HURT MINDS,* GREAT NATURE'S SECOND COURSE, *CHIEF NOURISHER* IN *LIFE'S FEAST;*

WHAT DO YOU *MEAN?*

STILL IT CRIED, *'SLEEP NO MORE!'* TO ALL THE HOUSE: GLAMIS HATH *MURDER'D* SLEEP, AND THEREFORE *CAWDOR* SHALL SLEEP NO MORE; *MACBETH* SHALL SLEEP NO MORE!

35

Act Two
Scene Three

The porter is woken by the knocking at the castle gate...

Here's a knocking, indeed! If a man were porter of *hell-gate*, he should have old turning the key.

BANG! BANG!

Knock, knock, knock. *Who's there*, i' the name of Beelzebub?

Here's a *Farmer*, that *hanged* himself on the *expectation of plenty:* come in time; have *napkins* enough about you; here you'll *sweat* for't.

BANG! BANG!

Knock, knock. *Who's there*, i' the *other* devil's name? -- 'Faith, here's an *equivocator*, that could swear in *both* the scales against *either* scale; who committed *treason* enough for *God's* sake, yet could not equivocate to *heaven:* O, *come in*, equivocator.

BANG! BANG!

Knock, knock, knock. Who's there? -- 'Faith, here's an *English tailor* come hither, For stealing out of a *French hose:* come in, tailor; here you may *roast your goose.*

BANG! BANG!

Knock, knock. Never at *quiet!* What *are* you? -- But this place is too *cold* for hell. I'll *devil-porter* it no *further:* I had thought to have let in some of *all* professions, that go the primrose way to the *everlasting bonfire.*

BANG! BANG!

ANON, ANON: I PRAY YOU, REMEMBER THE *PORTER.*

WAS IT *SO LATE*, FRIEND, ERE YOU WENT TO BED, THAT YOU DO *LIE* SO LATE?

'FAITH SIR, WE WERE CAROUSING TILL THE *SECOND COCK;* AND *DRINK*, SIR, IS A GREAT PROVOKER OF *THREE* THINGS.

WHAT THREE THINGS DOES DRINK ESPECIALLY PROVOKE?

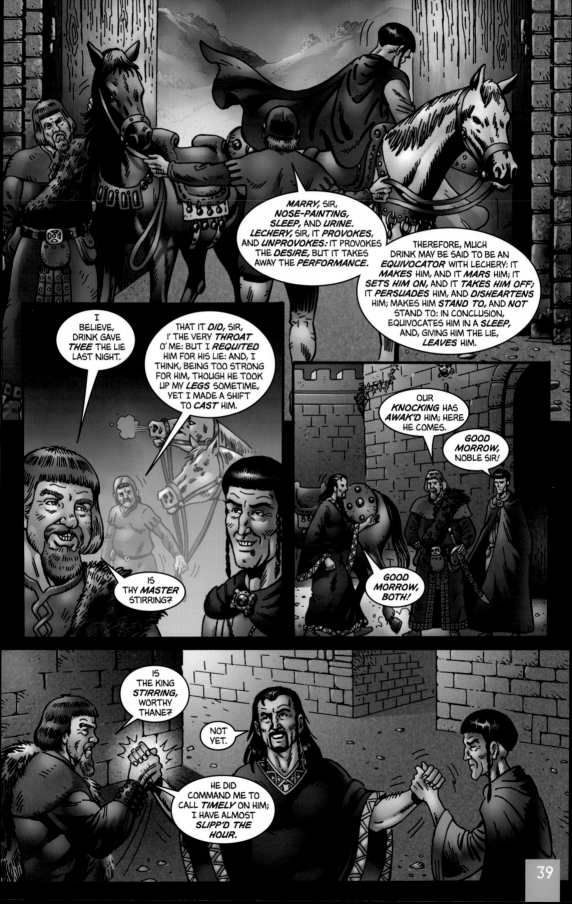

MARRY, SIR, NOSE-PAINTING, SLEEP, AND URINE. LECHERY, SIR, IT PROVOKES, AND UNPROVOKES: IT PROVOKES THE DESIRE, BUT IT TAKES AWAY THE PERFORMANCE.

THEREFORE, MUCH DRINK MAY BE SAID TO BE AN EQUIVOCATOR WITH LECHERY: IT MAKES HIM, AND IT MARS HIM; IT SETS HIM ON, AND IT TAKES HIM OFF; IT PERSUADES HIM, AND DISHEARTENS HIM; MAKES HIM STAND TO, AND NOT STAND TO: IN CONCLUSION, EQUIVOCATES HIM IN A SLEEP, AND, GIVING HIM THE LIE, LEAVES HIM.

I BELIEVE, DRINK GAVE THEE THE LIE LAST NIGHT.

THAT IT DID, SIR, I' THE VERY THROAT O' ME: BUT I REQUITED HIM FOR HIS LIE: AND, I THINK, BEING TOO STRONG FOR HIM, THOUGH HE TOOK UP MY LEGS SOMETIME, YET I MADE A SHIFT TO CAST HIM.

OUR KNOCKING HAS AWAK'D HIM; HERE HE COMES.

GOOD MORROW, NOBLE SIR!

IS THY MASTER STIRRING?

GOOD MORROW, BOTH!

IS THE KING STIRRING, WORTHY THANE?

NOT YET.

HE DID COMMAND ME TO CALL TIMELY ON HIM; I HAVE ALMOST SLIPP'D THE HOUR.

39

O!
BY WHOM?

THOSE OF HIS *CHAMBER,* AS IT SEEM'D, HAD DONE'T: THEIR *HANDS AND FACES* WERE ALL BADG'D WITH *BLOOD;* SO WERE THEIR *DAGGERS,* WHICH, UNWIP'D, WE FOUND UPON THEIR PILLOWS: THEY *STAR'D,* AND WERE *DISTRACTED;* NO MAN'S LIFE WAS TO BE TRUSTED WITH THEM.

O!
YET I DO REPENT ME OF MY *FURY,* THAT I DID *KILL* THEM.

WHEREFORE DID YOU SO?

WHO CAN BE WISE, AMAZ'D, TEMPERATE AND FURIOUS, LOYAL AND NEUTRAL, IN A MOMENT? *NO* MAN: THE EXPEDITION OF MY *VIOLENT LOVE* OUTRUN THE *PAUSER REASON.*

HERE LAY *DUNCAN,* HIS SILVER SKIN *LAC'D* WITH HIS *GOLDEN BLOOD;* AND HIS *GASH'D STABS* LOOK'D LIKE A *BREACH IN NATURE* FOR *RUIN'S* WASTEFUL ENTRANCE: THERE, THE *MURDERERS,* STEEP'D IN THE COLOURS OF THEIR TRADE, THEIR DAGGERS UNMANNERLY BREECH'D WITH GORE. WHO COULD *REFRAIN,* THAT HAD A HEART TO LOVE, AND IN THAT HEART *COURAGE,* TO MAKE'S LOVE KNOWN?

44

LET'S BRIEFLY PUT ON *MANLY READINESS,* AND MEET I' THE *HALL* TOGETHER.

WELL CONTENTED.

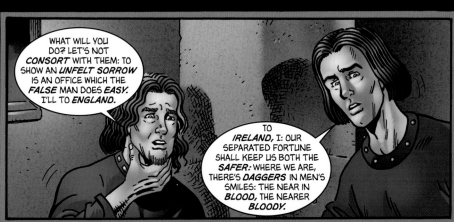

WHAT WILL YOU DO? LET'S NOT *CONSORT* WITH THEM: TO SHOW AN *UNFELT SORROW* IS AN OFFICE WHICH THE *FALSE* MAN DOES *EASY.* I'LL TO *ENGLAND.*

TO *IRELAND,* I: OUR *SEPARATED FORTUNE* SHALL KEEP US BOTH THE *SAFER:* WHERE WE ARE, THERE'S *DAGGERS* IN MEN'S SMILES: THE NEAR IN *BLOOD,* THE NEARER *BLOODY.*

THIS *MURDEROUS SHAFT* THAT'S SHOT HATH NOT YET *LIGHTED,* AND OUR SAFEST WAY IS TO *AVOID THE AIM:* THEREFORE, *TO HORSE;* AND LET US NOT BE DAINTY OF *LEAVE-TAKING,* BUT *SHIFT AWAY.* THERE'S *WARRANT* IN THAT THEFT WHICH STEALS ITSELF, WHEN THERE'S NO *MERCY* LEFT.

47

Macbeth is now King of Scotland. In the King's Palace at Forres, Banquo is suspicious...

TAN-TARA!

TAN-TARA!

HERE'S OUR *CHIEF GUEST*.

IF HE HAD BEEN *FORGOTTEN*, IT HAD BEEN AS A *GAP* IN OUR *GREAT FEAST*, AND ALL-THING UNBECOMING.

THOU HAST IT *NOW*, KING, CAWDOR, GLAMIS, ALL, AS THE *WEIRD WOMEN* PROMIS'D, AND, I FEAR, THOU PLAY'DST MOST *FOULLY* FOR'T; YET IT WAS SAID, IT SHOULD NOT STAND IN THY *POSTERITY*; BUT THAT MYSELF SHOULD BE THE *ROOT* AND *FATHER* OF *MANY KINGS*. IF THERE COME *TRUTH* FROM THEM, -- AS UPON *THEE*, MACBETH, THEIR SPEECHES *SHINE*, -- WHY, BY THE VERITIES ON THEE MADE GOOD, MAY THEY NOT BE *MY* ORACLES AS WELL, AND SET ME UP IN HOPE?

BUT HUSH; *NO MORE*.

TO-NIGHT WE HOLD A *SOLEMN SUPPER*, SIR, AND I'LL REQUEST YOUR *PRESENCE*.

LET YOUR HIGHNESS *COMMAND* UPON ME, TO THE WHICH MY DUTIES ARE WITH A MOST *INDISSOLUBLE TIE* FOR EVER KNIT.

LET EVERY MAN BE *MASTER* OF HIS TIME TILL *SEVEN AT NIGHT,* TO MAKE SOCIETY THE *SWEETER WELCOME:* WE WILL KEEP *OURSELF* TILL SUPPER-TIME *ALONE:* WHILE THEN, *GOD BE WITH YOU.*

SIRRAH, A *WORD* WITH YOU.

ATTEND THOSE *MEN* OUR PLEASURE?

THEY *ARE,* MY LORD, WITHOUT THE *PALACE* GATE.

BRING THEM *BEFORE* US.

TO BE THUS IS *NOTHING,* BUT TO BE *SAFELY* THUS. -- OUR *FEARS* IN BANQUO STICK *DEEP,* AND IN HIS *ROYALTY* OF NATURE REIGNS THAT WHICH WOULD BE *FEAR'D:* 'TIS MUCH HE *DARES;*

AND, TO THAT DAUNTLESS TEMPER OF HIS MIND, HE HATH A WISDOM THAT DOTH GUIDE HIS *VALOUR* TO ACT IN *SAFETY.* THERE IS NONE BUT *HE* WHOSE BEING I DO FEAR: AND UNDER HIM MY *GENIUS* IS *REBUK'D;* AS, IT IS SAID, *MARK ANTONY'S* WAS BY *CAESAR.*

HE *CHID* THE SISTERS, WHEN FIRST THEY PUT THE NAME OF KING UPON ME, AND BADE THEM SPEAK TO *HIM;* THEN *PROPHET-LIKE,* THEY HAIL'D *HIM* FATHER TO A *LINE OF KINGS.*

51

UPON MY HEAD THEY PLAC'D A *FRUITLESS CROWN,* AND PUT A *BARREN SCEPTRE* IN MY GRIPE, THENCE TO BE WRENCH'D WITH AN *UNLINEAL HAND,* NO SON OF MINE SUCCEEDING. IF 'T BE SO, FOR *BANQUO'S ISSUE* HAVE I FIL'D MY MIND;

THUMP!!!

FOR *THEM* THE GRACIOUS *DUNCAN* HAVE I MURDER'D; PUT *RANCOURS* IN THE VESSEL OF MY PEACE, ONLY FOR *THEM;* AND MINE ETERNAL JEWEL GIVEN TO THE COMMON ENEMY OF MAN, TO MAKE *THEM* KINGS, THE *SEED OF BANQUO* KINGS! RATHER THAN SO, *COME, FATE,* INTO THE LIST, AND *CHAMPION* ME TO THE *UTTERANCE!*

WHO'S THERE!

NOW, GO TO THE *DOOR,* AND STAY THERE TILL WE *CALL.*

WAS IT NOT *YESTERDAY* WE SPOKE TOGETHER?

IT *WAS,* SO PLEASE YOUR HIGHNESS.

WELL THEN, NOW -- HAVE YOU *CONSIDER'D* OF MY SPEECHES?

KNOW, THAT IT WAS *HE*, IN THE TIMES PAST, WHICH HELD YOU SO *UNDER FORTUNE*, WHICH, YOU THOUGHT, HAD BEEN OUR *INNOCENT SELF.*

THIS I MADE *GOOD* TO YOU IN OUR LAST CONFERENCE; PASS'D IN *PROBATION* WITH YOU, HOW YOU WERE *BORNE IN HAND;* HOW *CROSS'D;* THE *INSTRUMENTS;* WHO WROUGHT *WITH* THEM; AND ALL THINGS ELSE, THAT MIGHT, TO HALF A SOUL, AND TO A NOTION CRAZ'D SAY, '*THUS DID BANQUO.*'

YOU MADE IT *KNOWN* TO US.

I *DID* SO; AND WENT *FURTHER*, WHICH IS NOW OUR POINT OF *SECOND* MEETING. DO YOU FIND YOUR *PATIENCE* SO PREDOMINANT IN YOUR NATURE, THAT YOU CAN *LET THIS GO?*

ARE YOU SO *GOSPELL'D* TO PRAY FOR THIS GOOD MAN, AND FOR HIS ISSUE, WHOSE *HEAVY HAND* HATH BOW'D YOU TO THE *GRAVE*, AND *BEGGAR'D* YOURS FOR EVER?

WE *ARE* MEN, MY LIEGE.

AY, IN THE *CATALOGUE* YE GO FOR MEN; AS *HOUNDS,* AND *GREYHOUNDS, MONGRELS, SPANIELS, CURS, SHOUGHS, WATER-RUGS,* AND *DEMI-WOLVES,* ARE CLEPT ALL BY THE NAME OF *DOGS:*

THE *VALU'D FILE* DISTINGUISHES THE *SWIFT,* THE *SLOW,* THE *SUBTLE,* THE *HOUSEKEEPER,* THE *HUNTER,* EVERY ONE ACCORDING TO THE *GIFT* WHICH BOUNTEOUS NATURE HATH IN HIM CLOS'D; WHEREBY HE DOES RECEIVE PARTICULAR ADDITION, FROM THE BILL THAT WRITES THEM ALL ALIKE; AND SO OF *MEN.*

NOW, IF *YOU* HAVE A STATION IN THE FILE, NOT I' THE WORST RANK OF MANHOOD, *SAY'T;* AND I WILL PUT THAT *BUSINESS* IN YOUR BOSOMS, WHOSE EXECUTION TAKES YOUR *ENEMY* OFF, GRAPPLES YOU TO THE *HEART* AND *LOVE* OF US, WHO WEAR OUR HEALTH BUT *SICKLY* IN *HIS* LIFE, WHICH IN HIS *DEATH* WERE *PERFECT.*

I AM ONE, MY LIEGE, WHOM THE *VILE BLOWS* AND *BUFFETS* OF THE WORLD HAVE SO *INCENS'D,* THAT I AM RECKLESS WHAT I DO, TO *SPITE* THE WORLD.

AND I *ANOTHER,* SO *WEARY* WITH *DISASTERS,* TUGG'D WITH *FORTUNE,* THAT I WOULD SET MY LIFE ON *ANY* CHANCE, TO *MEND* IT, OR BE *RID* ON'T.

BOTH OF YOU KNOW, *BANQUO* WAS YOUR *ENEMY.*

TRUE, MY LORD.

SO IS *MINE;* AND IN SUCH *BLOODY DISTANCE,* THAT EVERY *MINUTE* OF HIS BEING THRUSTS AGAINST MY *NEAR'ST OF LIFE:*

AND THOUGH I COULD WITH *BARE-FAC'D POWER* SWEEP HIM FROM MY SIGHT, AND BID MY WILL *AVOUCH* IT, YET I MUST *NOT,* FOR CERTAIN *FRIENDS* THAT ARE BOTH *HIS* AND *MINE,* WHOSE *LOVES* I MAY NOT DROP, BUT WAIL HIS FALL WHO I *MYSELF* STRUCK DOWN: AND THENCE IT IS THAT I TO *YOUR* ASSISTANCE DO MAKE LOVE, *MASKING* THE BUSINESS FROM THE *COMMON EYE,* FOR SUNDRY WEIGHTY REASONS.

WE *SHALL,* MY LORD, PERFORM WHAT YOU *COMMAND* US.

THOUGH OUR *LIVES*—

YOUR *SPIRITS* SHINE *THROUGH* YOU.

54

WITHIN THIS *HOUR,* AT MOST, I WILL ADVISE YOU WHERE TO *PLANT* YOURSELVES, ACQUAINT YOU WITH THE PERFECT *SPY O' THE TIME,* THE *MOMENT* ON'T; FOR'T MUST BE DONE *TO-NIGHT,* AND SOMETHING FROM THE *PALACE;* ALWAYS THOUGHT, THAT I REQUIRE A *CLEARNESS:*

AND *WITH* HIM, -- TO LEAVE NO *RUBS* NOR *BOTCHES* IN THE WORK, -- *FLEANCE* HIS *SON,* THAT KEEPS HIM COMPANY, WHOSE *ABSENCE* IS NO LESS MATERIAL TO ME THAN IS HIS *FATHER'S,* MUST EMBRACE THE FATE OF THAT *DARK HOUR.*

RESOLVE YOURSELVES *APART:* I'LL COME TO YOU *ANON.*

WE *ARE* RESOLV'D, MY LORD.

I'LL CALL UPON YOU *STRAIGHT:* ABIDE WITHIN.

IT IS *CONCLUDED:* BANQUO, THY *SOUL'S FLIGHT,* IF IT FIND *HEAVEN,* MUST FIND IT OUT *TO-NIGHT.*

DUNCAN IS IN HIS *GRAVE;* AFTER LIFE'S FITFUL FEVER HE SLEEPS WELL; *TREASON* HAS DONE HIS *WORST:* NOR STEEL, NOR POISON, MALICE DOMESTIC, FOREIGN LEVY, *NOTHING* CAN TOUCH HIM FURTHER!

SO *SHALL* I, LOVE; AND SO, I PRAY, BE *YOU.* LET YOUR *REMEMBRANCE* APPLY TO BANQUO: PRESENT HIM *EMINENCE,* BOTH WITH *EYE* AND *TONGUE:* UNSAFE THE WHILE, THAT WE MUST LAVE OUR HONOURS IN THESE FLATTERING STREAMS, AND MAKE OUR FACES *VISARDS* TO OUR HEARTS, *DISGUISING* WHAT THEY ARE.

COME ON; *GENTLE* MY LORD, SLEEK O'ER YOUR RUGGED LOOKS; BE *BRIGHT* AND *JOVIAL* AMONG YOUR GUESTS TO-NIGHT.

YOU MUST *LEAVE* THIS.

O! FULL OF *SCORPIONS* IS MY MIND, DEAR WIFE! THOU *KNOW'ST* THAT BANQUO, AND HIS FLEANCE, *LIVES.*

BUT IN THEM NATURE'S COPY'S NOT *ETERNE.*

THERE'S *COMFORT* YET; THEY ARE *ASSAILABLE:* THEN BE THOU *JOCUND.* ERE THE *BAT* HATH FLOWN HIS CLOISTER'D FLIGHT; ERE TO *BLACK HECATE'S SUMMONS* THE *SHARD-BORNE BEETLE,* WITH HIS DROWSY HUMS, HATH RUNG NIGHT'S YAWNING PEAL, THERE SHALL BE DONE A DEED OF *DREADFUL NOTE.*

57

WHAT'S TO BE *DONE?*

COME, SEELING NIGHT, SCARF UP THE TENDER EYE OF PITIFUL DAY, AND, WITH THY BLOODY AND INVISIBLE HAND, *CANCEL,* AND *TEAR TO PIECES,* THAT *GREAT BOND* WHICH KEEPS ME *PALE!*

LIGHT *THICKENS;* AND THE *CROW* MAKES WING TO THE *ROOKY WOOD;* GOOD THINGS OF DAY BEGIN TO *DROOP* AND *DROWSE,* WHILES *NIGHT'S BLACK AGENTS* TO THEIR *PREYS* DO ROUSE.

BE *INNOCENT* OF THE KNOWLEDGE, DEAREST CHUCK, TILL THOU *APPLAUD* THE DEED.

THOU *MARVELL'ST* AT MY WORDS: BUT HOLD THEE *STILL;* THINGS *BAD* BEGUN MAKE *STRONG* THEMSELVES BY ILL. SO, PR'YTHEE, *GO* WITH ME.

64

65

THOU CANST NOT SAY *I* DID IT: NEVER SHAKE THY *GORY LOCKS* AT ME.

SIT, WORTHY FRIENDS. MY LORD IS *OFTEN* THUS, AND HATH BEEN FROM HIS *YOUTH:* PRAY YOU, *KEEP SEAT;* THE FIT IS *MOMENTARY:* UPON A *THOUGHT* HE WILL AGAIN BE *WELL.* IF MUCH YOU *NOTE* HIM, YOU SHALL *OFFEND* HIM AND EXTEND HIS *PASSION; FEED,* AND *REGARD* HIM *NOT.*

GENTLEMEN, *RISE:* HIS HIGHNESS IS *NOT WELL.*

Are you a *man?*

Ay, and a *bold* one, that dare look on that which might *appal the devil.*

O proper stuff! This is the very *painting* of your *fear:* this is the *air-drawn dagger,* which, you said, led you to *Duncan. O!* these Flaws and starts, -- impostors to true fear, -- would well become a *woman's story* at a *winter's fire,* authoris'd by her *grandam. Shame itself!*

AVAUNT! AND *QUIT MY SIGHT!* LET THE *EARTH* HIDE THEE! THY BONES ARE *MARROWLESS,* THY BLOOD IS *COLD;* THOU HAST NO *SPECULATION* IN THOSE EYES, WHICH THOU DOST GLARE WITH.

CRASHHHH!!!

THINK OF THIS, GOOD PEERS, BUT AS A *THING OF CUSTOM:* 'TIS NO OTHER; ONLY IT SPOILS THE *PLEASURE* OF THE TIME.

WHAT *MAN* DARE, *I* DARE: APPROACH THOU LIKE THE *RUGGED RUSSIAN BEAR,* THE *ARM'D RHINOCEROS,* OR THE *HYRCAN TIGER;* TAKE *ANY* SHAPE BUT *THAT,* AND MY FIRM NERVES SHALL NEVER TREMBLE: OR BE *ALIVE* AGAIN, AND DARE ME TO THE DESERT WITH THY *SWORD;*

IF *TREMBLING* I INHABIT THEN, PROTEST ME THE *BABY OF A GIRL.*

HENCE, HORRIBLE SHADOW! UNREAL MOCKERY, HENCE!

I WILL TO-MORROW -- AND BETIMES I WILL -- TO THE *WEIRD SISTERS: MORE* SHALL THEY SPEAK;

FOR NOW I AM BENT TO KNOW, BY THE *WORST MEANS,* THE *WORST.* FOR MINE OWN GOOD, ALL CAUSES SHALL GIVE WAY: I AM IN *BLOOD* STEPP'D IN SO FAR, THAT, SHOULD I WADE NO MORE, *RETURNING* WERE AS TEDIOUS AS GO O'ER. STRANGE THINGS I HAVE IN HEAD, THAT WILL TO HAND, WHICH MUST BE *ACTED,* ERE THEY MAY BE *SCANN'D.*

YOU LACK THE SEASON OF ALL NATURES, *SLEEP.*

COME, WE'LL TO SLEEP. MY STRANGE AND SELF-ABUSE IS THE *INITIATE FEAR,* THAT WANTS *HARD USE:* WE ARE YET BUT *YOUNG* IN DEED.

74

On the battlements of the Kings Palace, two Scottish thanes are concerned...

MY *FORMER SPEECHES* HAVE BUT HIT YOUR *THOUGHTS*, WHICH CAN INTERPRET *FURTHER:* ONLY, I SAY, THINGS HAVE BEEN *STRANGELY BORNE.*

THE GRACIOUS *DUNCAN* WAS PITIED OF MACBETH: -- MARRY, HE WAS *DEAD:* -- AND THE RIGHT-VALIANT *BANQUO* WALK'D TOO LATE; WHOM, YOU MAY SAY, IF'T PLEASE YOU, *FLEANCE* KILL'D, FOR FLEANCE *FLED.*

MEN MUST NOT WALK TOO LATE. WHO CANNOT WANT THE THOUGHT, HOW *MONSTROUS* IT WAS FOR *MALCOLM,* AND FOR *DONALBAIN,* TO KILL THEIR GRACIOUS FATHER? *DAMNED FACT!*

HOW IT DID *GRIEVE* MACBETH! DID HE NOT *STRAIGHT,* IN *PIOUS RAGE,* THE TWO *DELINQUENTS* TEAR, THAT WERE THE SLAVES OF *DRINK,* AND THRALLS OF *SLEEP?*

WAS NOT THAT *NOBLY* DONE? AY, AND *WISELY* TOO; FOR 'TWOULD HAVE ANGER'D *ANY HEART ALIVE* TO HEAR THE MEN *DENY* IT.

SO THAT, I SAY, HE HAS BORNE ALL THINGS *WELL:* AND I DO THINK, THAT, HAD HE *DUNCAN'S SONS* UNDER HIS KEY, -- AS, AN'T PLEASE HEAVEN, HE *SHALL NOT,* -- THEY SHOULD FIND WHAT 'TWERE TO *KILL A FATHER;* SO SHOULD *FLEANCE.*

BUT, *PEACE!* -- FOR FROM BROAD WORDS, AND 'CAUSE HE FAIL'D HIS PRESENCE AT THE TYRANT'S FEAST, I HEAR, *MACDUFF* LIVES IN *DISGRACE.* SIR, CAN YOU TELL WHERE HE *BESTOWS* HIMSELF?

THE *SON OF DUNCAN,* FROM WHOM THIS TYRANT HOLDS THE DUE OF BIRTH, LIVES IN THE *ENGLISH COURT;* AND IS RECEIV'D OF THE MOST PIOUS *EDWARD* WITH SUCH GRACE, THAT THE MALEVOLENCE OF FORTUNE NOTHING TAKES FROM HIS HIGH RESPECT. THITHER *MACDUFF* IS GONE TO PRAY THE *HOLY KING,* UPON HIS AID TO WAKE *NORTHUMBERLAND,* AND WARLIKE *SIWARD:*

THAT, BY THE HELP OF THESE, -- WITH *HIM ABOVE* TO *RATIFY* THE WORK, -- WE MAY AGAIN GIVE TO OUR TABLES *MEAT, SLEEP* TO OUR *NIGHTS,* FREE FROM OUR FEASTS AND BANQUETS *BLOODY KNIVES,* DO *FAITHFUL HOMAGE,* AND RECEIVE *FREE HONOURS,* ALL WHICH WE *PINE* FOR NOW.

AND THIS REPORT HATH SO *EXASPERATE* THE KING, THAT HE PREPARES FOR SOME ATTEMPT OF *WAR.*

SENT HE TO *MACDUFF?*

HE *DID:* AND WITH AN ABSOLUTE *'SIR, NOT I,'* THE CLOUDY MESSENGER TURNS ME HIS *BACK,* AND *HUMS,* AS WHO SHOULD SAY 'YOU'LL *RUE* THE TIME THAT CLOGS ME WITH THIS ANSWER.'

AND THAT WELL MIGHT ADVISE HIM TO A *CAUTION,* TO HOLD WHAT *DISTANCE* HIS WISDOM CAN PROVIDE.

SOME *HOLY ANGEL* FLY TO THE COURT OF ENGLAND, AND UNFOLD HIS *MESSAGE* ERE HE COME, THAT A *SWIFT BLESSING* MAY SOON RETURN TO THIS OUR SUFFERING COUNTRY UNDER A *HAND ACCURS'D!*

I'LL SEND MY *PRAYERS* WITH HIM.

85

87

WHEN WE HOLD *RUMOUR* FROM WHAT WE FEAR, YET KNOW NOT *WHAT* WE FEAR, BUT FLOAT UPON A *WILD AND VIOLENT SEA*, EACH WAY, AND MOVE.

I TAKE MY *LEAVE* OF YOU: SHALL NOT BE LONG BUT I'LL BE *HERE* AGAIN. THINGS AT THE *WORST* WILL *CEASE*, OR ELSE *CLIMB UPWARD* TO WHAT THEY WERE *BEFORE*.

MY PRETTY COUSIN, *BLESSING* UPON YOU!

FATHER'D HE IS, AND YET HE'S *FATHERLESS*.

I AM SO MUCH A *FOOL*, SHOULD I STAY *LONGER*, IT WOULD BE MY *DISGRACE*, AND YOUR *DISCOMFORT*: I TAKE MY LEAVE AT ONCE.

SIRRAH, YOUR FATHER'S *DEAD*: AND WHAT WILL YOU DO *NOW*? HOW WILL YOU *LIVE*?

AS *BIRDS* DO, MOTHER.

WHAT, WITH *WORMS AND FLIES*?

WITH WHAT I *GET*, I MEAN; AND SO DO *THEY*.

POOR BIRD! THOU'DST *NEVER* FEAR THE *NET*, NOR *LIME*, THE *PIT-FALL*, NOR THE *GIN*.

WHY *SHOULD* I, MOTHER? POOR BIRDS THEY ARE NOT *SET* FOR.

89

BLEED, BLEED, POOR COUNTRY! GREAT TYRANNY, LAY THOU THY BASIS SURE, FOR *GOODNESS* DARE NOT *CHECK* THEE! *WEAR* THOU THY WRONGS; THE *TITLE* IS *AFFEER'D!*

FARE THEE WELL, LORD: I WOULD NOT BE THE *VILLAIN* THAT THOU THINK'ST FOR THE *WHOLE SPACE* THAT'S IN THE *TYRANT'S GRASP,* AND THE RICH *EAST* TO BOOT.

BE NOT OFFENDED: I SPEAK NOT AS IN *ABSOLUTE* FEAR OF YOU.

I THINK OUR COUNTRY *SINKS* BENEATH THE *YOKE;* IT *WEEPS,* IT *BLEEDS;* AND EACH NEW DAY A *GASH* IS ADDED TO HER *WOUNDS:* I *THINK,* WITHAL, THERE WOULD BE *HANDS* UPLIFTED IN MY *RIGHT;*

AND *HERE,* FROM *GRACIOUS ENGLAND,* HAVE I OFFER OF *GOODLY THOUSANDS:*

BUT, FOR ALL THIS, WHEN I SHALL *TREAD* UPON THE TYRANT'S *HEAD,* OR *WEAR* IT ON MY *SWORD,* YET MY POOR COUNTRY SHALL HAVE *MORE VICES* THAN IT HAD *BEFORE,* MORE *SUFFER,* AND MORE *SUNDRY WAYS* THAN EVER, BY HIM THAT SHALL *SUCCEED.*

WHAT SHOULD HE BE?

IT IS *MYSELF* I MEAN: IN WHOM I KNOW ALL THE PARTICULARS OF *VICE* SO GRAFTED, THAT, WHEN THEY SHALL BE OPEN'D, BLACK *MACBETH* WILL SEEM AS *PURE AS SNOW;* AND THE POOR STATE ESTEEM HIM AS A *LAMB,* BEING COMPAR'D WITH MY *CONFINELESS HARMS.*

95

MACDUFF, THIS *NOBLE PASSION*, CHILD OF INTEGRITY, HATH FROM MY SOUL *WIP'D* THE *BLACK SCRUPLES*, RECONCIL'D MY THOUGHTS TO THY *GOOD TRUTH* AND *HONOUR*.

DEVILISH MACBETH BY MANY OF THESE TRAINS HATH SOUGHT TO WIN ME INTO HIS *POWER*, AND *MODEST WISDOM* PLUCKS ME FROM *OVER-CREDULOUS HASTE*: BUT *GOD ABOVE* DEAL BETWEEN THEE AND ME!

FOR EVEN NOW I PUT MYSELF TO THY DIRECTION, AND *UNSPEAK* MINE OWN DETRACTION; HERE *ABJURE* THE TAINTS AND BLAMES I LAID UPON MYSELF, FOR *STRANGERS* TO MY NATURE.

I AM YET *UNKNOWN* TO WOMAN; *NEVER* WAS FORSWORN; SCARCELY HAVE *COVETED* WHAT WAS MINE *OWN*; AT NO TIME *BROKE MY FAITH*: WOULD NOT BETRAY THE *DEVIL* TO HIS FELLOW; AND DELIGHT NO LESS IN *TRUTH*, THAN *LIFE*: MY *FIRST* FALSE SPEAKING WAS THIS UPON *MYSELF*.

WHAT I AM *TRULY*, IS *THINE*, AND MY POOR *COUNTRY'S* TO *COMMAND*:

WHITHER, INDEED, BEFORE THY HERE-APPROACH, OLD *SIWARD*, WITH *TEN THOUSAND WARLIKE MEN*, ALREADY AT A POINT, WAS *SETTING FORTH*. NOW WE'LL *TOGETHER*, AND THE CHANCE OF *GOODNESS* BE LIKE OUR *WARRANTED QUARREL*!

An English doctor approaches...

WHY ARE YOU *SILENT*?

SUCH *WELCOME* AND *UNWELCOME* THINGS AT ONCE, 'TIS *HARD* TO *RECONCILE*.

WELL; MORE ANON.

COMES THE *KING* FORTH, I PRAY YOU?

AY, SIR; THERE ARE A CREW OF *WRETCHED SOULS*, THAT STAY HIS *CURE*: THEIR *MALADY* CONVINCES THE GREAT ASSAY OF ART; BUT AT HIS *TOUCH*, SUCH *SANCTITY* HATH HEAVEN GIVEN HIS HAND, THEY PRESENTLY *AMEND*.

I *THANK* YOU, DOCTOR.

ALAS, POOR COUNTRY! ALMOST AFRAID TO KNOW ITSELF. IT CANNOT BE CALL'D OUR MOTHER, BUT OUR GRAVE; WHERE NOTHING, BUT WHO KNOWS NOTHING, IS ONCE SEEN TO SMILE;

WHERE SIGHS, AND GROANS, AND SHRIEKS THAT RENT THE AIR, ARE MADE, NOT MARK'D; WHERE VIOLENT SORROW SEEMS A MODERN ECSTASY: THE DEAD MAN'S KNELL IS THERE SCARCE ASK'D FOR WHO; AND GOOD MEN'S LIVES EXPIRE BEFORE THE FLOWERS IN THEIR CAPS, DYING OR ERE THEY SICKEN.

O RELATION, TOO NICE, AND YET TOO TRUE!

WHAT IS THE NEWEST GRIEF?

THAT OF AN HOUR'S AGE DOTH HISS THE SPEAKER: EACH MINUTE TEEMS A NEW ONE.

HOW DOES MY WIFE?

WHY, WELL.

AND ALL MY CHILDREN?

WELL TOO.

THE TYRANT HAS NOT BATTER'D AT THEIR PEACE?

NO; THEY WERE WELL AT PEACE, WHEN I DID LEAVE THEM.

BUT NOT A NIGGARD OF YOUR SPEECH: HOW GOES IT?

WHEN I CAME HITHER TO TRANSPORT THE TIDINGS, WHICH I HAVE *HEAVILY* BORNE, THERE RAN A RUMOUR OF MANY *WORTHY FELLOWS* THAT WERE *OUT;* WHICH WAS TO MY BELIEF *WITNESS'D* THE RATHER, FOR THAT I SAW THE *TYRANT'S POWER* AFOOT.

NOW IS THE TIME OF *HELP.* YOUR *EYE* IN SCOTLAND WOULD CREATE *SOLDIERS,* MAKE OUR *WOMEN* FIGHT, TO *DOFF* THEIR *DIRE DISTRESSES.*

BE 'T THEIR COMFORT, WE ARE *COMING* THITHER. GRACIOUS *ENGLAND* HATH LENT US GOOD *SIWARD,* AND *TEN THOUSAND MEN;* AN *OLDER,* AND A *BETTER* SOLDIER, NONE THAT *CHRISTENDOM* GIVES OUT.

'WOULD I COULD *ANSWER* THIS COMFORT WITH THE LIKE! BUT I HAVE WORDS, THAT WOULD BE HOWL'D OUT IN THE *DESERT AIR,* WHERE *HEARING* SHOULD NOT *LATCH* THEM.

WHAT *CONCERN* THEY? THE *GENERAL* CAUSE? OR IS IT A FEE-GRIEF, DUE TO SOME *SINGLE* BREAST?

NO MIND THAT'S *HONEST* BUT IN IT SHARES SOME WOE, THOUGH THE *MAIN* PART PERTAINS TO *YOU ALONE.*

IF IT BE *MINE,* KEEP IT NOT *FROM* ME; QUICKLY LET ME *HAVE* IT.

LET NOT YOUR EARS *DESPISE* MY TONGUE FOR EVER, WHICH SHALL POSSESS THEM WITH THE *HEAVIEST SOUND,* THAT EVER YET THEY *HEARD.*

HUMPH! I *GUESS* AT IT.

Act Five
Scene One

Late at night in Dunsinane Castle...

I HAVE *TWO NIGHTS* WATCH'D WITH YOU, BUT CAN PERCEIVE NO *TRUTH* IN YOUR REPORT. WHEN WAS IT SHE *LAST WALK'D?*

SINCE HIS MAJESTY WENT INTO THE FIELD, I HAVE SEEN HER *RISE* FROM HER *BED*, THROW HER *NIGHT-GOWN* UPON HER, UNLOCK HER *CLOSET*, TAKE FORTH *PAPER*, FOLD IT, *WRITE* UPON IT, *READ* IT, AFTERWARDS *SEAL* IT, AND AGAIN RETURN TO *BED*; YET ALL THIS WHILE IN A MOST FAST *SLEEP.*

A GREAT *PERTURBATION* IN NATURE, TO RECEIVE AT ONCE THE BENEFIT OF *SLEEP*, AND DO THE EFFECTS OF *WATCHING*. IN THIS SLUMBERY AGITATION, BESIDES HER *WALKING* AND OTHER ACTUAL *PERFORMANCES*, WHAT, AT ANY TIME, HAVE YOU HEARD HER *SAY?*

THAT, SIR, WHICH I WILL NOT *REPORT* AFTER HER.

YOU MAY TO *ME*; AND 'TIS MOST *MEET* YOU *SHOULD.*

NEITHER TO *YOU* NOR *ANY ONE*; HAVING NO *WITNESS* TO *CONFIRM* MY SPEECH.

LO YOU, HERE SHE *COMES*. THIS IS HER *VERY GUISE*;

And, upon my life, *fast asleep*. Observe her: stand *close.*

Do you *mark* that?

THE THANE OF FIFE HAD A *WIFE*: WHERE IS SHE *NOW*?

WHAT, WILL THESE HANDS *NE'ER* BE CLEAN?

NO *MORE* O' THAT, MY LORD, NO *MORE* O' THAT: YOU *MAR* ALL WITH THIS *STARTING*.

Go to, go to: you have *known* what you should *not*.

She has *spoke* what she should not, I am sure of *that*: Heaven knows what she has *known*.

HERE'S THE SMELL OF THE *BLOOD* STILL: ALL THE PERFUMES OF *ARABIA* WILL NOT *SWEETEN* THIS LITTLE HAND.

OH! OH! OH!

What a *sigh* is there! The *heart* is *sorely* charg'd.

I would not have such a heart in *my* bosom, for the dignity of the *whole body*.

Well, well, well.

'Pray God, it *be*, sir.

This *disease* is *beyond my practice*: yet I have known those which have *walk'd in their sleep*, who have died *holily* in their beds.

WASH YOUR HANDS, PUT ON YOUR NIGHTGOWN; LOOK NOT SO PALE.

I TELL YOU YET AGAIN, BANQUO'S BURIED: HE CANNOT COME OUT ON'S GRAVE.

Even so?

TO BED, TO BED: THERE'S KNOCKING AT THE GATE. COME, COME, COME, COME, GIVE ME YOUR HAND. WHAT'S DONE CANNOT BE UNDONE.

TO BED, TO BED, TO BED.

WILL SHE GO NOW TO BED?

DIRECTLY.

FOUL WHISPERINGS ARE ABROAD. UNNATURAL DEEDS DO BREED UNNATURAL TROUBLES: INFECTED MINDS TO THEIR DEAF PILLOWS WILL DISCHARGE THEIR SECRETS. MORE NEEDS SHE THE DIVINE THAN THE PHYSICIAN.

GOD, GOD FORGIVE US ALL!

LOOK AFTER HER; REMOVE FROM HER THE MEANS OF ALL ANNOYANCE, AND STILL KEEP EYES UPON HER. SO, GOOD NIGHT: MY MIND SHE HAS MATED, AND AMAZ'D MY SIGHT. I THINK, BUT DARE NOT SPEAK.

GOOD NIGHT, GOOD DOCTOR.

GO, *PRICK THY FACE,* AND OVER-RED THY *FEAR,* THOU *LILY-LIVER'D* BOY.

WHAT SOLDIERS, PATCH? *DEATH OF THY SOUL!* THOSE *LINEN CHEEKS* OF THINE ARE COUNSELLORS TO *FEAR.*

WHAT SOLDIERS, WHEY-FACE?

THE *ENGLISH FORCE,* SO PLEASE YOU.

TAKE THY FACE HENCE.

SEYTON!

I AM SICK AT HEART, WHEN I BEHOLD--

SEYTON, I SAY!

THIS PUSH WILL *CHEER* ME EVER, OR *DISSEAT* ME NOW. I HAVE LIV'D LONG ENOUGH: MY WAY OF LIFE IS FALL'N INTO THE *SERE,* THE *YELLOW LEAF;*

AND THAT WHICH SHOULD *ACCOMPANY* OLD AGE, AS HONOUR, LOVE, OBEDIENCE, TROOPS OF FRIENDS, I MUST NOT LOOK TO *HAVE;* BUT, IN THEIR STEAD, *CURSES,* NOT LOUD, BUT DEEP, MOUTH-HONOUR, BREATH, WHICH THE POOR HEART WOULD FAIN *DENY,* AND DARE NOT.

113

I HAVE ALMOST *FORGOT* THE *TASTE OF FEARS.* THE TIME HAS BEEN, MY SENSES WOULD HAVE *COOL'D* TO HEAR A NIGHT-SHRIEK; AND MY FELL OF HAIR WOULD AT A *DISMAL TREATISE* ROUSE, AND STIR, AS *LIFE* WERE IN'T. I HAVE SUPP'D *FULL* WITH HORRORS: *DIRENESS,* FAMILIAR TO MY *SLAUGHTEROUS THOUGHTS,* CANNOT ONCE *START* ME.

Moments later...

WHEREFORE WAS THAT CRY?

THE *QUEEN,* MY LORD, IS *DEAD.*

SHE SHOULD HAVE DIED *HEREAFTER:* THERE WOULD HAVE BEEN A *TIME* FOR SUCH A WORD.

TO-MORROW, AND TO-MORROW, AND TO-MORROW, CREEPS IN THIS PETTY PACE FROM DAY TO DAY TO THE *LAST SYLLABLE* OF *RECORDED TIME; AND ALL OUR YESTERDAYS* HAVE LIGHTED *FOOLS* THE WAY TO *DUSTY DEATH.*

OUT, OUT, BRIEF CANDLE!

LIFE'S BUT A *WALKING SHADOW;* A *POOR PLAYER,* THAT *STRUTS* AND *FRETS* HIS HOUR UPON THE STAGE, AND THEN IS HEARD NO MORE: IT IS A TALE TOLD BY AN *IDIOT,* FULL OF *SOUND AND FURY,* SIGNIFYING *NOTHING.*

THOU COM'ST TO USE THY *TONGUE*; THY STORY *QUICKLY.*

GRACIOUS MY LORD, I SHOULD REPORT THAT WHICH I SAY I *SAW,* BUT KNOW NOT HOW TO *DO* IT.

WELL, SAY, SIR.

AS I DID STAND MY WATCH UPON THE HILL, I LOOK'D TOWARD *BIRNAM,* AND ANON, METHOUGHT, THE *WOOD* BEGAN TO *MOVE.*

LIAR, AND SLAVE!

LET ME ENDURE YOUR *WRATH,* IF'T BE NOT SO. WITHIN THIS *THREE MILE* MAY YOU SEE IT COMING; I SAY, A *MOVING GROVE.*

IF THOU SPEAK'ST FALSE, UPON THE *NEXT TREE* SHALT THOU *HANG ALIVE,* TILL *FAMINE* CLING THEE: IF THY SPEECH BE *SOOTH,* I CARE NOT IF THOU DOST FOR *ME* AS MUCH.

I *PULL* IN *RESOLUTION;* AND BEGIN TO *DOUBT* THE EQUIVOCATION OF THE *FIEND,* THAT LIES LIKE TRUTH: *'FEAR NOT,* TILL *BIRNAM WOOD* DO COME TO *DUNSINANE;'* AND NOW A WOOD COMES TOWARD DUNSINANE.

ARM, ARM, AND OUT!

IF THIS WHICH HE AVOUCHES DOES *APPEAR,* THERE IS NOR *FLYING HENCE,* NOR *TARRYING HERE.* I 'GIN TO BE *AWEARY* OF THE SUN, AND WISH THE ESTATE O' THE WORLD WERE NOW *UNDONE.*

RING THE ALARUM-BELL! BLOW, WIND! COME, WRACK! AT LEAST WE'LL DIE WITH HARNESS ON OUR BACK.

Macbeth

End

William Shakespeare

(c.1564 - 1616 AD)

National Portrait Gallery, London.

William Shakespeare is one of the most widely read authors and possibly the best dramatist ever to live. The actual date of his birth is not known, but traditionally April 23rd 1564 (St George's Day) has been his accepted birthday, as this was three days before his baptism. He died on the same date in 1616, aged fifty-two.

The life of William Shakespeare can be divided into three acts. The first twenty years of his life were spent in Stratford-upon-Avon where he grew up, went to school, got married and became a father. The next twenty-five years he spent as an actor and playwright in London; and he spent his last few years back in Stratford-upon-Avon, where he enjoyed his retirement in moderate wealth gained from his successful years in the theatre.

William was the eldest son of tradesman John Shakespeare and Mary Arden, and the third of eight children. His father was later elected mayor of Stratford, which was the highest post a man in civic politics could attain. In sixteenth-century England, William was lucky to survive into adulthood; syphilis, scurvy, smallpox, tuberculosis, typhus and dysentery shortened life expectancy at the time to approximately thirty-five years. The Bubonic Plague took the lives of many and was believed to have

been the cause of death for three of William's seven siblings.

Little is known of William's childhood, other than it is thought that he attended the local grammar school, where he studied Latin and English Literature. In 1582, at the age of eighteen, William married a local farmer's daughter, Anne Hathaway, who was eight years his senior and three months pregnant. During their marriage they had three children: Susanna, born on May 26th 1583 and twins, Hamnet and Judith, born on February 2nd 1585. Hamnet, William's only son, caught Bubonic Plague and died aged just eleven.

Five years into his marriage William moved to London and appeared in many small parts at The Globe Theatre, then one of the biggest

theatres in England. His first appearance in public as a poet was in 1593 with *Venus and Adonis* and again in the following year with *The Rape of Lucrece*. Six years later, in 1599, he became joint proprietor of The Globe Theatre.

When Queen Elizabeth died in 1603, she was succeeded by her cousin King James of Scotland. King James supported Shakespeare and his band of actors and gave them license to call themselves "The King's Men" in return for entertaining the court.

In just twenty-three years, between 1590 and 1613, William Shakespeare is attributed with writing thirty-eight plays, one-hundred-and-fifty-four sonnets and five poems. No original manuscript exists for any of his plays, so it is hard to accurately date them. However, from their contents and reports of the day it is believed that his first play was *The Taming of the Shrew* and that his last complete work was *Two Noble Kinsmen*, written two years before he died. The cause of his death remains unknown.

He was buried on April 25th 1616, two days after his death, at the Church of the Holy Trinity (the same Church where he had been baptised fifty-two years earlier). His gravestone bears these words, believed to have been written by William himself:-

> "Good friend for Jesus sake forbear,
> To dig the dust enclosed here!
> Blest be the man that spares these stones,
> And curst be he that moves my bones"

At the time of his death, William had substantial properties, which he bestowed on his family and associates from the theatre.

In his will he left his wife, the former Anne Hathaway, his second best bed!

William Shakespeare's last direct descendant died in 1670. She was his granddaughter, Elizabeth.

The Real Macbeth

(c.1005 - 1057 AD)

Macbeth is one of Shakespeare's most famous characters. It is a name that's known the whole world over; but many people don't realise that the story is linked to actual historical events — even though those events have been heavily embellished and altered for the sake of entertainment.

Shakespeare obtained his information about the real Macbeth from Raphael Holinshed's book, *The Chronicles of England, Scotland and Ireland*, published in 1574 (which Shakespeare used as a primary resource for all of his historical plays). Holinshed himself derived his information from a variety of sources, most notably Andrew of Wyntoun's *Orygynale Cronykil* ("Original Chronicle") which traces a history of Scotland from Biblical times, and Hector Boece's

Scotorum Historiae ("Scottish History"), published in 1526 and translated from Latin into English by John Bellenden in 1535.

Macbeth, or rather Mac Bethad as he would have been called, was King of Scotland from 1040 to 1057 (although in Shakespeare's play, his reign is made to appear significantly less than seventeen years). The name "Mac Bethad" means

"son of life", and is actually Irish, rather than Scottish in origin.

Eleventh century Scotland was a barbaric land; with war and ruthless slaughter being a fact of life. Survival depended on having a strong and capable local ruler or chieftain to protect both life and property. Such a leader would provide a strong paternalistic rule, guarding the family, community and land from all enemies.

Some of these enemies could be, and often were, collections of distant family members challenging the current leadership.

A number of local rulers would often unite under the nominal leadership of one "king" to promote their common interests and to wage war on other more distant clans. Interestingly, in those times, kings and rulers could name their own successor – it wasn't a privilege that was handed down from parent to eldest child as the monarchy operates today. However, family linkage tended to be respected and the title usually passed to a relative of the king – selected as being the one most suitable for immediate rule, and not necessarily the natural heir. Understandably, this selection process would have been challenged, especially by those individuals who felt that they had a greater right to become king than the person taking on the title. Such grievances were often dealt with or pre-empted by the murdering of family members judged unsuitable for power, to ensure that the "favourite" won the race.

Macbeth was the son of Findláech mac Ruaidrí (who was a High Steward of Moray) in the north of Scotland, around 1005. His mother's name is unknown, and indeed her own parentage is inaccurately recorded. It is uncertain whether she was the daughter of King

Kenneth II or of King Malcolm II. However, that is largely immaterial as whichever man was Macbeth's grandfather, would be a strong enough family link for him to make a claim for the throne.

In 1020, Macbeth's father Findláech died. It is thought that he was killed, most probably by his brother Máel Brigté's son Máel Coluim (Malcolm). Findláech's title of High Steward went to his nephew Gille Coemgáin. In 1032, Gille Coemgáin and fifty other people were burned to death as punishment for the murder of Findláech. This act of retribution could well have been carried out by

Macbeth and his allies. Following Gille Coemgáin's death, Macbeth took the title of High Steward of Moray.

It was around this time that he married Gille Coemgáin's widow, Gruoch, and became step-father to her son, Lulach (which explains why Shakespeare has Lady Macbeth talk about motherhood, whereas at no time does Macbeth make any reference to being a father. Moreover, Macduff states that Macbeth has no children in Act IV Scene III (page 102)). Macbeth's marriage to Gruoch was significant, because she was the grand-daughter of Kenneth III. Therefore through their combined

ancestors the marriage ensured that Macbeth had a strong claim to the throne.

Within a very short space of time, Macbeth's rival Gille Coemgáin had not only lost his life, but his title and his widowed wife had gone swiftly to Macbeth.

While Macbeth was a high-ranking lord of Moray, the King at the time was Donnchad mac Crináin (King Duncan I). Duncan succeeded to the throne when his grandfather, King Malcolm II died at Glamis. It is thought likely that Malcolm had engineered the position of Duncan taking over from him, through the tactical assassination of any family members who might feel they had a stronger claim to the crown.

Given the circumstances, it would have been a sensible course of action for Duncan to make peace with his remaining family, in particular his cousin Thorfinn the Mighty (Earl of Orkney), his cousin Macbeth, and the person closest to his throne in terms of lineage, namely Gruoch, the wife of Macbeth. Duncan appears to have been unsuccessful in uniting the "royal family", and Macbeth pressed his own claim to the throne with the help of that same cousin and ally, Earl Thorfinn of Orkney. He eventually won the crown by slaying Duncan at Bothgowanan near Elgin in 1040.

Macbeth has been judged by history to be a more able king than his predecessor. Under his rule the kingdom became relatively stable and reasonably prosperous, so much so, that by 1050 he was confident enough to leave the country for a number of months and make a pilgrimage to Rome. At this time he was said to have been so wealthy that he "scattered alms like seed corn". As Wyntoun's *Orygynale Cronykil* says:-

> "In pilgrimage þidder he come,
> And in almus he sew siluer"

All was not peaceful, however, and in 1054 Duncan I's son, Máel Coluim mac Donnchada (Malcolm Canmore, nicknamed "big head"), challenged Macbeth for the throne of Scotland. He did so in alliance with Siward, Earl of Northumbria (who also happened to be the cousin of Duncan's widow) and they took control of much of southern Scotland. Three years later, on 15 August 1057 Macbeth's army was finally defeated at the Battle of Lumphanan, in Aberdeenshire. Macbeth was killed in battle. He is believed to be buried in the graveyard at Saint Oran's Chapel on the Isle of Iona, the last of many Kings of Alba and Dalriada to be laid to rest there. This site is also supposed to be the final resting place of King Duncan I.

Unlike in Shakespeare's play, the killing of Macbeth didn't result in the crown going straight to Duncan's son Malcolm. It first went to Macbeth's step-son Lulach, on the basis that Kenneth III was his maternal great-grandfather. Lulach was a weak king and ridiculed, being called "Lulach the Simple" or "Lulach the Fool". After a few months of rule, he was murdered; and Malcolm, son of Duncan I, became King Malcolm III of Scotland.

No-one knows what happened to Lady Macbeth. Dramatically, Shakespeare has her losing her sanity and taking her own life – however there is no record of that happening, or even of her falling to a bloody death. Having lived through the murder of her first husband, the killing of her second husband in battle, and the murder of her son, even if she was to outlive them all, it's unlikely that she enjoyed any form of happiness.

Macbeth and the Kings of Scotland

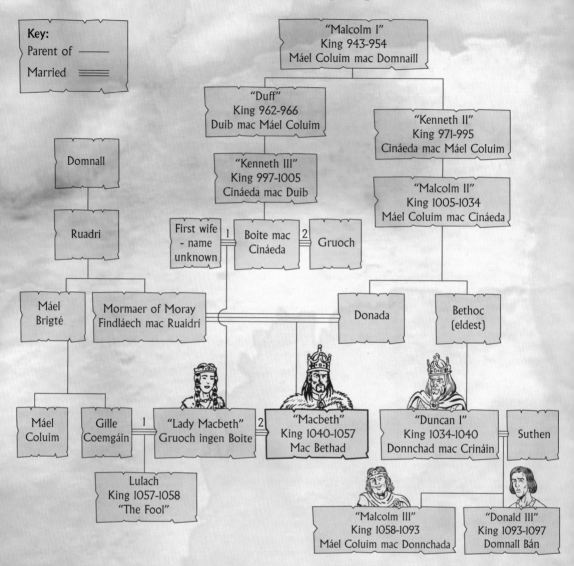

Key:

Parent of ————

Married ══════

"Malcolm I"
King 943-954
Máel Coluim mac Domnaill

"Duff"
King 962-966
Duib mac Máel Coluim

"Kenneth II"
King 971-995
Cináeda mac Máel Coluim

"Kenneth III"
King 997-1005
Cináeda mac Duib

"Malcolm II"
King 1005-1034
Máel Coluim mac Cináeda

Domnall

Ruadri

First wife – name unknown

1 Boite mac Cináeda 2 Gruoch

Máel Brigté

Mormaer of Moray
Findláech mac Ruaidrí

Donada

Bethoc (eldest)

Máel Coluim

Gille Coemgáin

1 "Lady Macbeth"
Gruoch ingen Boite 2

"Macbeth"
King 1040-1057
Mac Bethad

"Duncan I"
King 1034-1040
Donnchad mac Crináin

Suthen

Lulach
King 1057-1058
"The Fool"

"Malcolm III"
King 1058-1093
Máel Coluim mac Donnchada

"Donald III"
King 1093-1097
Domnall Bán

The Macbeth Murder Trail

1020 – Macbeth's father Findláech died – thought to have been killed by his own nephew, Máel Coluim. His title of High Steward went to Máel Coluim's brother, Gille Coemgáin.

1032 – Gille Coemgáin and 50 other people were burned to death as punishment for the killing of Findláech. Thought to have been carried out by Macbeth and his allies as retribution for killing his father. Macbeth takes his title (that had been his father's) and also takes Gille Coemgáin's widow, Gruoch, for his wife.

There is another theory, that Gille Coemgáin killed Boite mac Cináeda because he had made his wife the heiress to his estate. As retaliation for this murder, Boite's wife

Gruoch (the stepmother of the Gruoch that married Gille Coemgáin and later Macbeth) mustered an army to kill Gille Coemgáin.

1040 – Macbeth killed King Duncan I at Bothgowanan.

1050 – Macbeth went on a pilgrimage to Rome.

1054 – Máel Coluim mac Donnchada (Malcolm, son of King Duncan I) stakes his claim to the throne and challenges Macbeth in the first of a series of battles.

1057 – Macbeth's army is finally defeated by Malcolm's army at the Battle of Lumphanan. Macbeth is killed in battle. Macbeth's step-son Lulach becomes King.

1057 – After only a few months of rule, Malcolm kills Lulach and becomes King Malcolm III of Scotland.

The History of Shakespeare's Macbeth

When comparing the play to the actual historical events, it is clear that those events were merely inspiration for Shakespeare's own take on the story. It is unlikely that he deliberately intended to misrepresent the facts; however it is important to recognise that as a playwright, Shakespeare had a responsibility to entertain his audience with his works. Therefore, what takes place on the stage is an artistic modification of what took place in history; to give the best portrayal of the plots and motives of the characters in order to arrive at a worthy spectacle. Amongst other things, Shakespeare possessed good business sense — and a successful play would draw in the fee-paying public to provide him and his troupe with an income.

But money was not his sole concern. His position in society was paramount, and of prime importance was the need to pander to the monarch.

Macbeth is thought to have been written to be performed in honour of a royal visit by the King of Denmark to King James I in 1606. King James I became King of England in 1603 when Elizabeth I died. He was already King of Scotland (King James VI of Scotland). Interestingly, James I was a keen scholar, and had a deep interest in witchcraft; so much so that in 1597 he wrote a book on the subject which he called *Daemonologie* and in it he advocated that witches should be dealt with severely. In addition, he was a keen supporter of the arts, having the title of "The King's Men" bestowed upon Shakespeare's acting company soon after his coronation. In return, The King's Men were expected to perform at court whenever they were asked, which amounted to around a dozen performances each year.

Setting the play in Scotland and including elements of witchcraft appears to be a deliberate attempt by Shakespeare to please the new King. But he can't take the credit for including witchcraft in the tale of *Macbeth*: we have Holinshed to thank for that. Raphael Holinshed's *Chronicles of England, Scotland and Ireland*, first published in 1574, was a primary source of reference for a number of Shakespeare's plays, and *Macbeth* is no exception. The following extract from Holinshed's *Chronicles* demonstrates just how closely Shakespeare borrowed from his version of events:

"It fortuned as Makbeth and Banquho iournied towards Fores, where the king then laie, they went sporting by the waie togither without other company saue onelie themselues, passing thorough the woods and fields, when suddenlie in the middest of a laund, there met them three women in strange and wild apparell, resembling creatures of the elder world, whome when they attentiuelie beheld, woondering much at the sight, the first of them spake and said: All haile Makbeth, thane of Glammis (for he had latelie entered into that dignitie and office by the death of his father Sinell). The second of them said: Haile Makbeth thane of Cawder. But the third said: All haile Makbeth that heereafter shalt be king of Scotland.

Then Banquho: What manner of women (saith he) are you, that seeme so little fauourable vnto me, whereas to my fellow heere, besides high offices, ye assigne also the kingdome, appointing foorth nothing for me at all? Yes, (saith the first of them) we promise greater benefits vnto thee, than vnto him, for he shall reigne in deed, but with an vnluckie end: neither shall he leaue anie issue behind him to succeed in his place, where contrarilie thou in deed shalt not reigne at all, but of thee those shall be borne which shall gouern the Scotish kingdome by long order of continuall descent. Herewith the foresaid women vanished immediatlie out of their sight."

In those days, the Stuart Kings of Scotland (King James I was a Stuart) were believed to have descended from Banquo (this is unproven but may have some truth in it). The witches "predicted" a long line of kings and this is dealt with in the play verbally in Act I Scene III (page 15), and visually in Act IV Scene I (page 85) when Macbeth is shown a large number of kings in a line, that all bear a resemblance to Banquo. The "bloodline" is only made possible by Fleance escaping when his father is attacked. Holinshed describes how Walter Steward, the founder of the Stuart royal family, who married the daughter of Robert Bruce was a descendent of Fleance and therefore Banquo. This ancestral connection must have been behind a change that Shakespeare made to Holinshed's accounts, namely that in Holinshed, Banquo was an accomplice in Duncan's murder; to show an ancestor of the King to have acted unlawfully would have

been rather foolhardy on Shakespeare's part. Other pandering includes the reference to the English King (Edward the Confessor) having God-given powers to cure "the evil" in Act IV Scene III (page 99), also known as Scrofula. Edward was believed to have that power, and King James I revived the custom of sufferers being "touched" by the monarch as a cure for it.

But it is with his portrayal of the witches where Shakespeare really aimed to please the King. In his book, King James denounced witchcraft absolutely. It was his belief that witches were mostly women who had masculine features, typified by facial hair. They were in league with the devil, could summon up spirits, and could even curse images of people to control their destiny. These were early days in the understanding of witchcraft, and the very subject was a threat to King James' belief of divine right of kingship. In his world,

witchcraft was a devil-based display of evil that was an ever-present challenge to the sanctity of his God-given ruling. It is a general fear of witchcraft, then, that is the possible reason why neither Holinshed nor Shakespeare ever refer to the women as witches. In fact, the elements of witchcraft that exist in the play, particularly the spells and the appearance of Hecate, are now believed to be later additions, made by Thomas Middleton following on from his own play, "The Witch". The term only appears once, in Act I Scene III (page 12*) and even then it could be an insult being reported by the speaker.

Beyond the belief that it was written for the visit of the King of Denmark in 1606, a number of other elements point towards it being authored in that year. The Porter's ramblings in Act II Scene III (page 38*) make mention of equivocation:

"O, come in, equivocator", which is thought to refer to the verbal cunning displayed by Father Garnet, one of the Gunpowder Plot conspirators in his trial of 1606. Also that year, a ship called The Tiger returned to England after a terrible two year voyage — and that ship is named in Act I Scene III (page 12*). However, as the first printed version of the play didn't appear until the Folio printing in 1623, the true dating and authenticity of each of the parts of the play are difficult to establish. For certain, a version of the play was first performed at The Globe Theatre in April 1611.

The Scottish Play

Macbeth is steeped in superstition; so much so that actors consider it the height of bad luck to even utter the name, unless they are rehearsing it at the time. Often, people will make references to "The Bard's Play" or "The Scottish Play" simply to avoid saying the "M"-word. There are a number of theories about the origins of the "curse" of *Macbeth*:

- It is thought that the witches' incantations are taken from real rituals and are believed to cast actual spells on the players.
- Legend has it that in 1606, Hal Berridge, the boy playing Lady Macbeth (remember that all the parts, male and female, were played by males at the time) died backstage.
- Another gruesome legend reports how in 1672 an actor playing the part of Macbeth substituted a real dagger for the blunt stage one, and actually killed the actor playing King Duncan in full view of the audience.

The more rational explanations are easier to accept.

- The majority of the play takes place in darkly lit scenes, and this tended to lead to a lot of accidents backstage.
- Yet another theory is that because *Macbeth* is a short play, and is so well known, that theatre groups would perform the play when they were in some financial trouble. Of course, a single play is rarely enough to save an ailing company, and therefore the performance of *Macbeth* became associated with failure, misery, and being out of work.

Whether any of those reasons are true or not is open to much speculation; what is beyond any doubt is that the story of *Macbeth* is a powerful, timeless tale of ambition, of the evil that is embedded in ill-gotten gains, and a question that lies at the heart of life itself — are we all the subjects of fate and destiny? Or do we carve out our own existence on this planet?

Page Creation

I n order to create three versions of the same book, the play is first adapted into three scripts: Original Text, Plain Text and Quick Text. While the degree of complexity changes for the dialogue in each script, the artwork remains the same for all three books.

On the left is a rough thumbnail sketch of page 73 created from the script (below). Once the rough sketch is approved it is redrawn as a clean finished pencil sketch (right).

ACT 3 – SCENE 5			
249. Somewhere far beyond the light of the sun, the three Witches huddle. Strange weather and strange landscapes surround them. They sense the approach of Hecate, the Queen of Darkness and they're frightened.			
250. BIG. Suddenly she's there! Hecate appears as a triple goddess, with three heads (women's in this frame, all identical, harsh-looking, but not ugly) and three bodies, standing back-to-back. She towers over the three Witches, piercing the gloom with her fierce stare. They cringe and make frightened animal noises.			
	QUICK TEXT	**PLAIN ENGLISH TEXT**	**ORIGINAL TEXT**
WITCHES (2 & 3)	WHIMPER! WHINE!	WHIMPER! WHINE!	WHIMPER! WHINE!
1ST WITCH	Hecate…you look angry.	Hecate! You look so angry.	Why, how now, Hecate! you look angerly.
HECATE	I am! You dared to meddle with Macbeth In riddles and affairs of death	Have I not reason, chaos that you are, Impertinent and rash? How did you dare To trade and traffic with Macbeth, In riddles, and affairs of death;	Have I not reason, beldams as you are, Saucy, and overbold? How did you dare To trade and traffic with Macbeth, In riddles, and affairs of death;
251. BIGish. The Witches scuttle round Hecate like dogs round their master. Hecate's three heads metamorphose into the heads of a horse, a dog and a boar.			
HECATE	You did it without me! And now I clearly see That all you've managed to do Is use him as he has used you.	And I, the mistress of your charms, The true instrument of all harms, Was never called to play my part. Or show the glory of our art? And, which is worse, all you have done Was only for a wayward son, Spiteful, and hateful; who, as others do, Wants all he can get and nought for you.	And I, the mistress of your charms, The close contriver of all harms, Was never call'd to bear my part. Or show the glory of our art? And, which is worse, all you have done Hath been but for a wayward son, Spiteful, and wrathful; who, as others do, Loves for his own ends, not for you.

From the pencil sketch an inked version of the same page is created (right).

Inking is not simply tracing over the pencil sketch, it is the process of using black ink to fill in the shaded areas and to add clarity, cohesion, depth and texture to the "pencils".

The "inks" give us the final outline which is checked for accuracy before being passed on to the colourist.

138

Adding colour brings the page and its characters to life.

Each character has a detailed character study drawn. This is useful for the artists to refer to and ensures continuity throughout the book.

Macbeth character study

The last stage of page creation is to add the speech bubbles and any sound effects.

Speech bubbles are created from the words in the script and are laid over the finished coloured artwork.

Three versions of lettering are produced for the three different versions of *Macbeth*. These are then saved as final artwork pages and compiled into separate books for printing.

Original Text

Plain Text

Quick Text

Shakespeare Around the Globe

The Globe Theatre and Shakespeare

It is hard to appreciate today how theatres were actually a new idea in William Shakespeare's time. The very first theatre in Elizabethan London to only show plays, aptly called "The Theatre", was introduced by an entrepreneur by the name of James Burbage. In fact, "The Globe Theatre", possibly the most famous theatre of that era, was built from the timbers of "The Theatre". The landlord of "The Theatre" was Giles Allen, who was a Puritan that disapproved of theatrical entertainment. When he decided to enforce a huge rent increase in the winter of 1598, the theatre members dismantled the building piece by piece and shipped it across the Thames to Southwark for reassembly. Allen was powerless to do anything, as the company owned the wood - although he spent three years in court trying to sue the perpetrators!

The report of the dismantling party (written by Schoenbaum) says:

"ryotous... armed... with divers and manye unlawfull and offensive weapons... in verye ryotous outragious and forcyble manner and contrarye to the lawes of your highnes Realme... and there pulling breaking and throwing downe the sayd Theater in verye outragious violent and riotous sort to the great disturbance and terrefyeing not onlye of your subjectes... but of divers others of your majesties loving subjectes there neere inhabitinge."

William Shakespeare became a part owner of this new Globe Theatre in 1599. It was one of four major theatres in the area, along with the Swan, the Rose, and the Hope. The exact physical structure of the Globe is unknown, although scholars are fairly sure of some details through drawings from the period. The theatre itself was a closed structure with an open courtyard where the stage stood. Tiered galleries around the open area accommodated the wealthier patrons who could afford seats, and those of the lower classes - the "groundlings" - stood around the platform or 'thrust' stage during the performance of a play. The space under and behind the stage was used for special effects, storage and costume changes. Surprisingly, although the entire structure was not very big by modern standards, it is known to have accommodated fairly large crowds - as many as 3,000 people - during a single performance.

The Globe II

In 1613, the original Globe Theatre burned to the ground when a cannon shot during a performance of *Henry VIII* set fire to the thatched roof of the gallery. Undeterred, the company completed a new Globe (this time with a tiled roof) on the foundations of its predecessor. Opened in 1614, Shakespeare didn't write any new plays for this theatre. He retired to Stratford-Upon-Avon that year, and died two years later. Despite that, performances continued until 1642, when the Puritans closed down all theatres and places of entertainment. Two years later, the Puritans razed the building to the ground in order to build tenements upon the site. No more was to be seen of the Globe for 352 years.

Shakespeare's Globe

Led by the vision of the late Sam Wanamaker, work began on the construction of a new Globe in 1993, close to the site of the original theatre. It was completed three years later, and Queen Elizabeth II officially opened the New Globe Theatre on June 12th, 1997 with a production of *Henry V*.

The New Globe Theatre is as faithful a reproduction as possible to the Elizabethan theatre, given that the details of the original are only known from sketches of the time. The building can accommodate 1,500 people between the galleries and the "groundlings".

www.shakespeares-globe.org

There are also replica Globe theatres in Rome and Berlin and The Old Globe in San Diego. In New York, ambitious plans are underway to convert a decaying military fortification, built to defend America against the British in the War of 1812, into a New Globe — and amazingly, the existing structure has an identical footprint to Shakespeare's Globe Theatre in London.

New Globe Theater, New York

Shakespeare Today

Our fascination with William Shakespeare has not diminished over the centuries. Despite being written over 400 years ago, his plays are still read in schools, adapted into graphic novels(!), made into films, performed in theatres the world over, and are still taken to the public by acting troupes, such as **the British Shakespeare Company**. The tradition of open-air theatre is deeply rooted in British culture. For over a thousand years companies have created theatres in the centre of towns, erecting a pageant wagon or scaffolding stage from which to perform great historical and classical drama for a mass audience. These open-air acting troupes, which weathered the theatrical shifts from medieval Mystery and Morality plays towards the sophisticated characterisation of Elizabethan drama, were the inspiration behind the British Shakespeare Company. The pageant wagons, and later inn-yards and amphitheatres outside London, were for centuries the only means by which Shakespeare and others could communicate with audiences beyond the capital. Today, more than 100,000 people watch BSC performances each year. With a full company of players and performances that feature original live music and songs, beautiful period costumes and the magic of a summer's evening, the BSC is fulfilling that primary aim of all performers throughout the years: to enchant and delight audiences of all classes and ages. **www.britishshakespearecompany.com**

The Lord Chamberlain's Men are another open-air performance troupe, with the interesting, but authentic twist that all the parts are played by men (as was the case in Shakespeare's day). **www.tcm.co.uk**

On the other side of the Atlantic, New York has Shakespeare in the Park. Since 1962, The Public Theater has staged productions of Shakespeare at The Delacorte Theater in Central Park. These performances are seen by approximately 80,000 New Yorkers and visitors each summer. In fact, since its inception, many of today's most acclaimed actors have taken part, including Patrick Stewart, Morgan Freeman, Meryl Streep, Denzel Washington, Kevin Kline and Jeff Goldblum. **www.publictheater.org**

Since 1997, Shakespeare 4 Kidz have been successfully providing an education in Shakespeare to children and young people all over the UK, and across the globe. Their unique approach has proved a hit with kids and adults alike. Their musicals have brought The Bard's work to life for thousands of people, and their creative education package is used extensively by teachers and education authorities throughout the UK. **www.shakespeare4kidz.com**

It seems that whatever time brings to our global society, and whatever developments take place within our cultures, William Shakespeare continues to have a place in our hearts and in our lives.

AVAILABLE IN THREE TEXT FORMATS

Macbeth:
The Graphic Novel
Original Text

ISBN:
978-1-906332-03-7

THE COMPLETE PLAY TRANSLATED INTO PLAIN ENGLISH!

THE UNABRIDGED ORIGINAL PLAY BROUGHT TO LIFE IN FULL COLOUR!

Macbeth:
The Graphic Novel
Plain Text

ISBN:
978-1-906332-04-4

THE FULL PLAY IN QUICK MODERN ENGLISH FOR A FAST-PACED READ!

Macbeth:
The Graphic Novel
Quick Text

ISBN:
978-1-906332-05-1

CHOOSE FROM ONE OF THREE TEXT FORMATS, ALL USING THE SAME HIGH QUALITY ARTWORK:

Original Text

This is the full, original script - just as The Bard intended. This version is ideal for purists, students and for readers who want to experience the unaltered text; all of the text, all of the excitement!

Plain Text

We take the original script and "convert" it into modern English, verse-for-verse. If you've ever wanted to fully appreciate the works of Shakespeare, but find the original language rather cryptic, then this is the version for you!

Quick Text

A revolution in graphic novels! We take the dialogue and reduce it to as few words as possible, but still retain the full essence of the story. This version allows readers to enter into and enjoy the stories quickly.

Classical Comics

Bringing Classics to Life

Classical Comics is a UK publisher creating graphic novel adaptations of literary classics. Faithful to the original vision of the authors, our books have been further enhanced by using only the finest artists - giving you a truly wonderful reading experience that you'll return to again and again.

LOOK OUT FOR MORE TITLES IN THE CLASSICAL COMICS RANGE

Original Text
978-1-906332-06-8

Quick Text
978-1-906332-08-2

September 2008

Jane Eyre: The Graphic Novel

This Charlotte Brontë classic is brought to vibrant life by artist John M. Burns. His sympathetic treatment of Jane Eyre's life during the 19th century will delight any reader with its strong emotions and wonderfully rich atmosphere. Travel back to a time of grand mansions contrasted with the severest poverty and immerse yourself in this fabulous love story.

Original Text
978-1-906332-15-0

Quick Text
978-1-906332-16-7

September 2008

Frankenstein: The Graphic Novel

True to the original novel (rather than the square-headed Boris Karloff image from the films!) Declan Shalvey's gothic artistic style is a perfect match for this epic tale. Frankenstein is such a well known name, yet the films strayed so far beyond the original novel that many people today don't realize how this classic horror tale deals with such timeless subjects as alienation, empathy and understanding beyond appearance.

Original Text
978-1-906332-17-4

Quick Text
978-1-906332-18-1

October 2008

A Christmas Carol: The Graphic Novel

A full-colour graphic novel adaptation of the much-loved Christmas story from the great Charles Dickens. Set in Victorian England and highlighting the social injustice of the time, we see one Ebenezer Scrooge go from oppressor to benefactor when he gets a rude awakening to how his life is, and how it should be. With sumptuous artwork and wonderful characters, this magical tale is a must-have for the festive season.

Original Text
978-1-906332-09-9

Quick Text
978-1-906332-11-2

January 2009

Great Expectations: The Graphic Novel

Charles Dickens' wonderful tale of Pip, Miss Havisham, and the spiteful Estella is retold here with fresh enthusiasm contained within Victorian ambience. Told through the eyes of the main character, Pip, we follow his fortunes from boyhood to adulthood as he experiences life in the 1800s - and has a few surprises along the way!

OTHER CLASSICAL COMICS TITLES:

The Tempest Published: May 2009
Original Text 978-1-906332-29-7
Plain Text 978-1-906332-30-3
Quick Text 978-1-906332-31-0

Romeo & Juliet Published: July 2009
Original Text 978-1-906332-19-8
Plain Text 978-1-906332-20-4
Quick Text 978-1-906332-21-1

Dracula Published: September 2009
Original Text 978-1-906332-25-9
Quick Text 978-1-906332-26-6

The Canterville Ghost Published: October 2009
Original Text..................................978-1-906332-27-3
Quick Text 978-1-906332-28-0

Sweeney Todd Published: January 2010
Original Text..................................978-1-906332-79-2
Quick Text 978-1-906332-80-8

For more information visit www.classicalcomics.com

Cover designs for illustration purposes only.